A SPEED BUMP & SLINGSHOT
MISADVENTURE

NIGHT
OF THE
LIVING
SHADOWS

Dave Coverly

Christy Ottaviano Books

Henry Holt and Company ✦ New York

Henry Holt and Company, LLC
Publishers since 1866
175 Fifth Avenue
New York, New York 10010
mackids.com

Library of Congress Cataloging-in-Publication Data is available.
ISBN 978-0-8050-8887-8

Our books may be purchased in bulk for promotional, educational, or business use.
Please contact your local bookseller or the Macmillan Corporate and Premium Sales Department
at (800) 221-7945 ext. 5442 or by e-mail at MacmillanSpecialMarkets@macmillan.com.

First Edition—2016
Printed in the United States of America by
R. R. Donnelley & Sons Company, Harrisonburg, Virginia

1 3 5 7 9 10 8 6 4 2

For every librarian who's ever helped a kid
find a new favorite book,
and for every kid who's ever asked a librarian
for help finding a new favorite book

CONTENTS

2

After his daring adventure rescuing his brother, Early Bird, from the evil Nightcrawlers, Speed Bump had been so exhausted that he fell asleep while flying.

Luckily for him, he'd been right over a forest of soft Yellowwood trees and didn't even wake up when he landed. Slingshot put his buddy on his back and flew him all the way home.

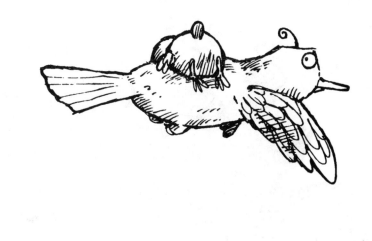

Speed Bump hadn't even so much as twitched when Slingshot dropped him into his nest, stuck the headphones over his ears, and turned on Birdthoven's Symphony no. 7 in Beak-Flat Major.

But now that Speed Bump was awake, Slingshot had more important things on his mind.

"Aren't you STARVING? I can hardly go 48 MINUTES without eating!" Slingshot groaned.

"Not really. I still sort of have that nasty Nightcrawler taste in my mouth."

"Mmmm, Nightcrawlers . . . Well, I HAD to get you up. Today's the scavenger hunt, remember?"

Speed Bump and Slingshot were members of the Bird Scouts. It was their favorite club, and it was where the two of them had met when they were little, before their fuzzy baby feathers had even developed into flight feathers. They'd done all their activities together and earned all their Bird Badges except for one: the Scavenger Badge.

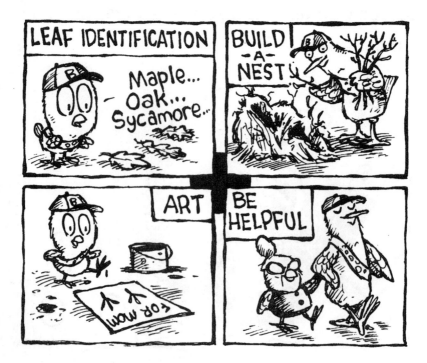

"Cheesable mercy, Slingshot! Is the scavenger hunt TODAY?"

"You bet! Why do you think I brought this stylish fanny pack?"

Slingshot put on his fanny pack while Speed Bump searched under his nest for his.

12

14

15

Then Speed Bump and Slingshot ran around the room, wings out, pretending to soar and trying to shriek like eagles. Mostly they just sounded like squeaky toys, but they didn't care.

ONE

CHAPTER THAT'S NUTS

"Boy, I thought finding something that turns would be a lot easier than this," Slingshot said as the friends circled over a field.

They'd been flying for so long that Slingshot had already stopped twice to eat some roly-poly bugs and a few yellow berries that were extremely sour.

Dotted against the sky were rows of birds sitting on wires, all cheeping and chirping and chattering about nothing in particular. Bird gossip, mostly. Speed Bump and Slingshot squeezed in between a couple of raspy-voiced Blue Jays.

Blue Jays were not known
for their social skills.

"We're, uh, on a scavenger hunt," said Speed Bump.

"What's a scavenger? How do you hunt it?"

"Do you have weapons? Is your weapon in that funny little pouch around your big waist?"

SNIFF
SNIFF
SNIFF

BEWARE OF SCAVENGER!

24

Excuse me, are you Nuthatch?
Yep, yep, yep! What's shakin'? Are you new here? You're new here, right? 'Cause I know EVERYONE on the wire and I don't know YOU! What're your names? I'm Nuthatch, yes sirree Bob, but my friends just call me Nuts. You can call me Nuts, too. I'm sure we'll be good friends very, very soon!

28

They flew together, following the
wire and passing telephone pole after
telephone pole. Sometimes Nuts and
Slingshot had to fly a little slower so
Speed Bump could catch up.

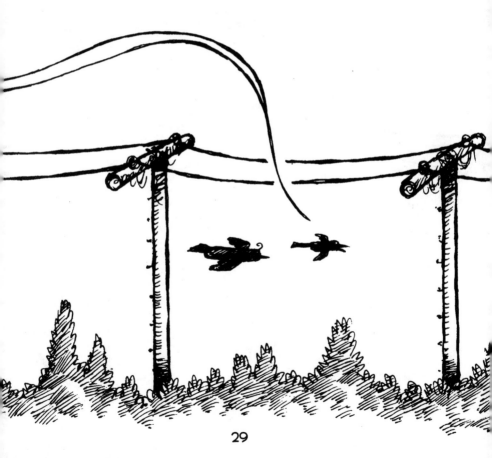

"Not to worry, my new friends," Nuts replied as they swerved around a wind turbine. "The place I'm taking you to has

EVERYTHING."

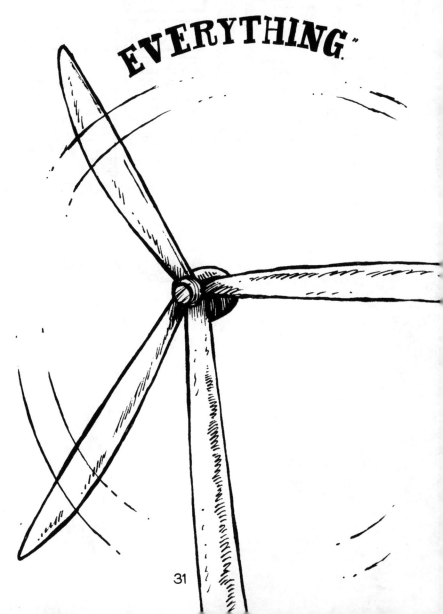

33

"They call it the mall. I'm not sure what it's for, but I like it. People come here to collect things—they walk in with no bags and walk out with lots of them, and they're all full! I'm telling you, they've got EVERYTHING here. You'll find more scavenger hunt stuff than you can shake a tail feather at!"

"Whoa," the friends said. They tried to high-five each other, but it was more of a low five because Speed Bump's wing didn't reach above his head.

TWO

CHAPTER
WITH STORES

"**A**nd the best part? There's food! Tons and tons of food! I mean, look at the people! Look how much they eat! Have you ever tried bread crumbs? You HAVE to try bread crumbs. Now, there's a meal that'll stick to your birdcage. But we'd better get in there fast. I think I just heard thunder!" Nuts looked up at the sky. It was cloudless.

"That was my stomach," Slingshot said proudly.

"Impressive. Okay, stay right behind me. I know a way to get inside."

"But it looks completely open!" Speed Bump said. "Why can't we just fly through the main entrance?"

"Oh, no no no no no," Nuts said. The feathers on his face quivered. "NEVER try to fly right in. It LOOKS open, but it's a trick. An evil trick! Those are called windows. Just because you can SEE through them doesn't mean you can GET through them. Believe me—I've made that mistake too many times!"

Speed Bump and Slingshot followed Nuts down to the front of the mall and landed on top of a trash can.

"This big window is really a door. Now we wait for people to open it so we can fly through. Not just one person, though— that doesn't give you enough time." Nuts shuddered at a memory. "When a bunch of people go in together, we go in with them, straight and fast, right over their heads."

41

As soon as they were inside, Speed
Bump let go of Slingshot's tail feathers,
and they flew to the top of a statue in
the center of the mall.

·OUR FOUNDER·
U.B. SPENDINMORE

Nuts gestured grandly with his wing.

"Take a gander around you, boys. More goodies than you could ever need!"

"This place is crazy!" said Speed Bump.

"Where do we even begin our scavenger hunt?" asked Slingshot.

"Good question, good question," said Nuts. "I see people looking at that board a lot. Maybe it will help."

They stared and stared at the directory.

"Nope."

"I got nothin'."

"Well, let's just start at the top of that moving stairs contraption."

MASSAGE CHAIR

TRY IT!

BIRKENSTORK

Then they ate and ate and ate until they could barely fly to the ceiling rafters.

But they were too late.

THREE

CHAPTER WITH GUTS

They flew down the corridors and checked every door. All of them were locked tight, and besides, the three birds weren't big enough to push them open anyway.

EMERGENCY EXIT
· ALARM WILL SOUND ·
DON'T EVEN THINK ABOUT IT!

Suddenly, the mall didn't seem quite
so fun. In fact, it seemed kind of scary.

61

CREEPY, you say? HA·HA·HA!

A grimy, disheveled bird with sticky-looking feathers popped up from the garbage can next to them. Speed Bump screamed and jumped into Slingshot's arms, and Nuts jumped onto his back.

"You outside birds don't know what you're MISSING! All these smells!" The bird held a half-eaten taco to his beak. "All these STORES! Look around! It's like this stuff is surrounding you and giving you a giant, squeezy hug and making you feel SAFE! Not like the outside, no sir!"

"I got trapped, too!" the bird said. "I escaped, but then I got trapped again! And again! And then I started to LIKE it! I mean, REALLY like it! And now I'll NEVER leave! NEVER! HA-HA-HA-HA-HA-HA-HA!" His eyes rolled back in his head as he laughed, and each eye looked in a different direction before they focused back on Speed Bump. Then the scrappy old bird scooped up a wing full of garbage.

The three of them flew to a nook in the rafters. Slingshot unzipped his fanny pack and pulled out three french fries.

"I really shouldn't, but . . ." said Nuts.

"How can you even think about eating when . . . yeah, okay, I'll take one," said Speed Bump.

A few minutes later, with bellies full
and beaks greasy, they were fast asleep.
Again.

FOUR

CHAPTER THAT'S GLASS

Sunlight streamed in through the mall skylight. Nuts ruffled his feathers and wiped his beak with a wing.

"It's open," he hollered. "Holy Crow, it's open! Let's GO!"

Speed Bump and Slingshot scrambled off the rafters and flew after Nuts as fast as they could, high above the morning shoppers and the smell of roasting coffee in the café. The birds spotted an older couple, wearing matching jogging suits, who were power walking straight toward the door outside.

THEM!

Speed Bump flapped his tiny wings as fast as he could, but it wasn't enough.

Slingshot, WAIT! Let me hold on to your tail!

But everything was happening too fast and Slingshot didn't hear his friend. He and Nuts zipped through the open door and up into the clear blue sky. Speed Bump was a second too late and flew headfirst into the glass.

Everything went blurry. He saw stars and worms around his head. Finally, Speed Bump came to his senses and realized he was sitting on the mall floor. His fanny pack had broken his fall.

Speed Bump began to panic. He didn't want to be alone. He didn't want to be stuck in the mall forever. And he DEFINITELY didn't want to live in a sticky garbage can and eat pork rinds every day.

He looked around for a place to hide.
That was when he saw a lady heading
for the exit. She had a big purse, and it
was unzipped. Maybe
it was his ticket
outside! He hopped
onto a short wall,
pushed off, and aimed
himself as straight as he
could toward the
opening.

HE MADE IT!

It was crowded inside the purse, and it smelled weird. Speed Bump was just about to pat himself on the back for his exit plan when he heard a horrible noise.

The lady was zipping her purse closed!

Speed Bump was wedged between strange objects as he bounced around in the dark. A door slammed. An engine roared. Music started playing on the radio. Then they were on the move.

FIVE

CHAPTER WITH WINGS

Outside the mall, Slingshot and Nuts had been watching through the glass door when Speed Bump flew into the lady's purse. They kept an eye on her and hovered above as she walked to her car.

Nuts started freaking out as the car drove away.

"Good plan, good plan!" said Nuts.

"I'd better, um, 'go'—*ahem*—you know!—on top of it so we don't forget which one it is."

"Now, that's using your head! Well, maybe not your head, exactly, but you know what I mean. . . ."

Slingshot cleared his throat.

After Slingshot was done marking the car, he and Nuts followed along, staying low so they wouldn't lose sight of it. The pair shot around stoplights, skimmed over street signs, and ducked under bridges as the lady drove toward the edge of the city.

"Uh-oh!" Nuts suddenly shouted over the traffic noise. "She's heading for the highway! We'll never keep up!"

Slingshot lowered his head, lifted his tail feathers, and zoomed down next to the car.

"I can see the purse in the backseat!
And the window's open! Just a little bit,
but I think I can squeeze through!"

"No, it's too dangerous! She's driving
really fast. You'll never time it right!"
Nuts squawked.

"I have to try—Speed Bump's my best friend! Plus he's TERRIBLE with directions! Even if he gets out of that purse, he'll NEVER find his way back to the forest!"

Slingshot flew furiously away from the car, which was already starting to accelerate as it approached the highway on-ramp. Then he circled around and headed straight for the back window.

With his eyes closed and the wind
pushing back the feathers on his face,
Slingshot flew into the window opening at
full speed.

He looked around and saw the wiggling
purse.

I did it! he thought.

Then he realized that only half of him was actually in the car. His bottom half was still outside, his tail feathers flapping like a flag in a stiff wind. He was stuck, his belly wedged against the top of the window.

Nuts rolled his eyes and muttered,
"What have I gotten myself into?" Then,
with a burst of energy, the Nuthatch
flew as fast as he could directly into
Slingshot's bulging backside.

With a loud squawk, the two birds tumbled onto the cushioned seat. They smoothed their feathers and looked around. Music was blaring from the radio; the lady hadn't seen or heard their sudden appearance.

Slingshot grabbed the zipper with his beak and pulled while Nuts held on to the strap. The purse slowly opened. Speed Bump's head popped out like he was hatching from an egg all over again.

At that very moment, the car came to a stop.

"Houses! It's a neighborhood!" Nuts whispered. "She's home! HIDE!"

The three of them dove into a pile of old food wrappers under the front seat.

The back door of the car opened, and
the lady reached in to grab her purse.

"GO!" Nuts hollered.

Wrappers went flying as the three
birds shot out from under the seat. The
lady screamed and dropped her purse.
Slingshot snatched some food as he
exited the car. None of them looked
back as they rose into the blue.

SIX

CHAPTER THAT DOESN'T RHYME WITH ANYTHING

"**W**ell, that was . . . um . . . interesting," Speed Bump said as he landed on the wire where Slingshot and Nuts were waiting.

"Yeah. Sure. Maybe." Speed Bump yawned. "Right now, though, I just want to go home and take a nap."

"Me too," Slingshot agreed, yawning himself. Then a pained look came over his face.

"*Au contraire, mon ami!*" Speed Bump said, using the only French words he had learned from Slingshot. "C'mon, follow me."

A huge smile appeared on Speed Bump's beak as he opened his overstuffed fanny pack.

114

SERIOUSLY, WE'RE OUT OF RHYMES

Back at Speed Bump's home, the buddies were swooping and screeching in celebration when Slingshot suddenly stopped and got a puzzled look on his face.

"Wait a minute. We were together almost the whole time at the mall! Where did you get all that stuff for the scavenger hunt?"

Speed Bump stopped and turned
to his friend. Slingshot paused, then
his eyes lit up.

"THE PURSE!"

they said together, laughing.

"Well, enough about treasures! I say we reward ourselves with some eagle food!" Slingshot declared. He flew out of the tree, and Speed Bump followed, doing his best to keep up.

Skweee!
Skweee!

Slingshot looked over
his wing and smiled.

Speed Bump sniffed the perfume trail as he followed his friend.

"Okay," he yelled. "But I don't think I'll have a problem finding you!"

Then the two of them swooped back down into the forest. Whatever happened next, they would be in it together.

Keep your eyes on the

skies for another

SPEED BUMP & SLINGSHOT
MISADVENTURE!